For my Mom, Janice, my Dad, Ray, and my Grandma Grace,
your love and support is a forever embrace — S. B. K.

To Vane, Ashley, and my father, with all my love — M. L.

My Mama Earth

Barefoot Books
294 Banbury Road
Oxford, OX2 7ED

Barefoot Books
2067 Massachusetts Ave
Cambridge, MA 02140

First published in Great Britain by Barefoot Books, Ltd and
in the United States of America by Barefoot Books, Inc in 2012

Interior design by Louise Millar, London
Reproduction by B & P International, Hong Kong
Printed in China on 100% acid-free paper
This book was typeset in Alana, Cochin and Twilight
The illustrations were prepared in gouache
paints on hot press paper

ISBN 978-1-84686-418-6

British Cataloguing-in-Publication Data:
a catalogue record for this book is available
from the British Library

Library of Congress Cataloging-in-Publication Data
is available under LCCN 2008051068

1 3 5 7 9 8 6 4 2

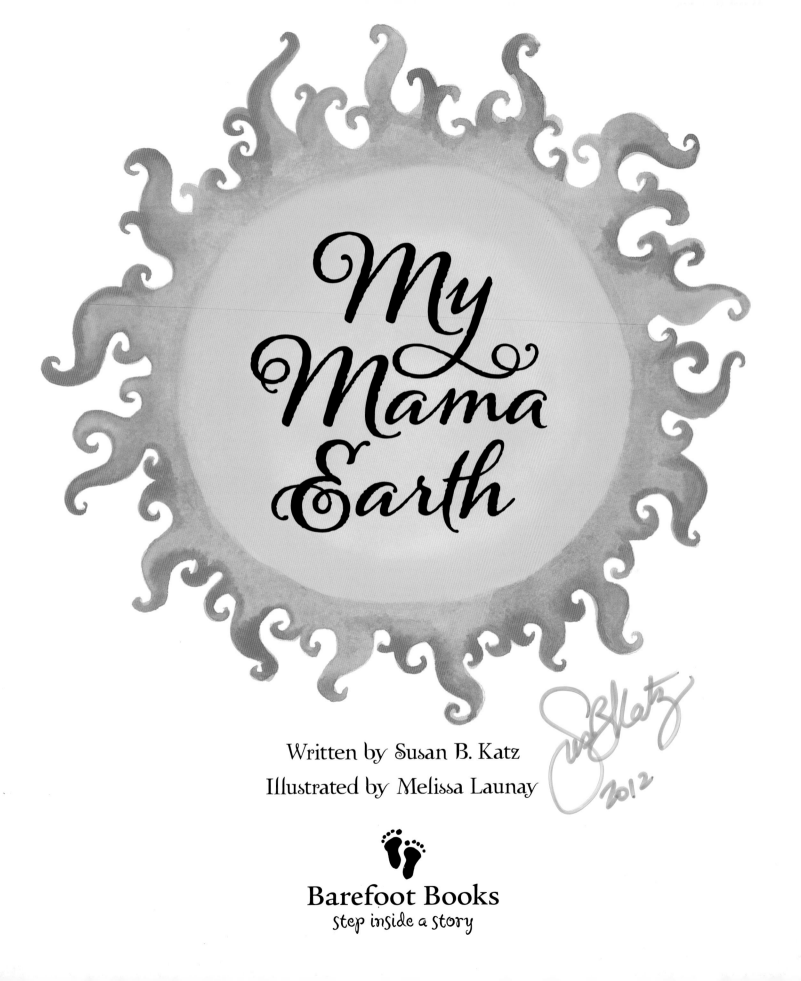

My Mama Earth

Written by Susan B. Katz

Illustrated by Melissa Launay

Barefoot Books

step inside a story

My mama wakes the eastern sun.
And weaves her magic till day's done.

My mama paints
the ocean creatures.

Adorning them with
brilliant features.

My mama sets the birds in flight.

She gives them nests to sleep at night.

My mama plants
the tiny seeds.

She grows the flowers,
pulls the weeds.

My mama makes
the hippos snore.

And mighty lions
proudly roar.

My mama shapes the forest trees.

Where gentle leaves caress the breeze.

My mama sets the sun out west.

And holds its warmth for when we rest.

My mama lights the millionth star.

Not too close, but not too far.

My mama hangs the moon for me.
She puts it low so I can see.

My mama sets her magic free.
And makes a warm, safe home for me.